**For Ma Boyle,
Teri, Kow, and Deebs**

BOLDER
FOR BOYS AND GIRLS
a frederator
mixed media group
company

Visit us on the Web! www.randomhouse.com/kids

Educators and librarians, for a variety of teaching tools, visit us at
www.randomhouse.com/teachers

Library of Congress Cataloging-in-Publication Data

Boyle, Bob.
Hugo and the really, really, really long string / by Bob Boyle. – 1st ed.
p. cm.
ISBN 978-0-375-83423-3 (trade) – ISBN 978-0-375-93423-0 (lib. bdg.)
Summary: Hugo follows a mysterious red string through his town, collecting a series of new
friends along the way, all of them knowing that something special must be at the end of the
string.
[1. String–Fiction. 2. Animals–Fiction.] I. Title.
PZ7.B69645Hu 2010
[E]–dc22
2006016303

MANUFACTURED IN MALAYSIA
10 9 8 7 6 5 4 3 2 1   First Edition

HUGO

and the really, really, really long string

by BOB BOYLE

Random House New York

In a little house on the top of a hill lived a happy little guy named Hugo and his playful dog, Biscuit.

One morning, Hugo was looking out his window
when what did he see . . .

. . . but a mysterious
red string!

Hugo just *knew* he would
find something wonderful at
the other end of it!

So Hugo followed the string through the trees,

down
a
hill,

across a river . . .

. . . and right up to a hole dug by Mrs. Mole!

Hugo sang out,
"My name is Hugo and I'm following this string!
As you can see, it's a wonderful thing!
There must be something special at the end!
I'll share it with you, my newfound friend!"

So down the hole they went!

Mrs. Mole led the way through the very long tunnel.

They popped out of another hole in the middle of the street. There they met Mr. Alligator Police!

Hugo and Mrs. Mole sang out,
"We are two friends who are following this string!
As you can see, it's a wonderful thing!
There must be something special at the end!
We'll share it with you, our newfound friend!"

So Mr. Alligator Police helped them follow the string
through the middle of town, down the street . . .

. . . through a noodle shop,

all the way back to the kitchen, and into a giant pot of Mr. Usagi's noodles!

Hugo, Mrs. Mole, and Mr. Alligator Police sang out,
"We are three friends who are following this string!
As you can see, it's a wonderful thing!
There must be something special at the end!
We'll share it with you, our newfound friend!"

So Mr. Usagi gave them each a bowl of noodles, and together they followed the string to the end of the block, up the stairs of the old schoolhouse,

and right into Mrs. Snake's classroom!

Hugo, Mrs. Mole, Mr. Alligator Police, and Mr. Usagi sang out,
"We are four friends who are following this string!
As you can see, it's a wonderful thing!
There must be something special at the end!
We'll share it with you, our newfound friend!"

Mrs. Snake and her students flew up high to point the way. Then they all hopped on a bus and traveled through the forest and up a winding road to the top of a hill.

Hugo thought this place looked familiar. When he
peeked over the bushes he saw . . .

. . . that the string led right back to his little house!

When Hugo followed the string to the end,
he got quite a surprise!

That mysterious red string wasn't special at all!

It was just a very long thread from his old underwear! It seems that Biscuit had carried her favorite new "toy" down the hill, through the tunnel, all through town, into the noodle shop, into the schoolhouse, through the forest, up the hill, and all the way back home again!

Hugo was disappointed . . . and EMBARRASSED!

But then everyone began to sing—
"We were eight strangers who followed the string!
It really was a wonderful thing!
There is something special where the string ends—
meeting new people we now call friends!"

So, after serving a snack of crumpets and tea . . .

Hugo said good night to his newfound friends, put on his favorite red pajamas . . .

. . . and, just like every night, went to sleep
with a smile on his face.